JODOROWSKY - BESS

THE WHITE LAMA

Translation: Justin Kelly

Book 5 - Open Hand, Closed Fist

Humanoids Publishing ™

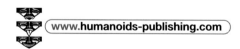

www.humanoids-publishing.com

Translation : Justin Kelly

Graphic design : Didier Gonord

Lettering : Kitof

THE WHITE LAMA
BOOK FIFTH - OPEN HAND, CLOSED FIST

English language edition © 2000 Humanoids Inc. Los Angeles, CA, USA.
Original French edition : Le Lama Blanc - La Quatrième Voix
© 2000 Les Humanoïdes Associés S.A. Geneva, Switzerland.
All rights reserved.

Humanoids Publishing
PO Box 931658
Hollywood, CA 90093

Printed in Belgium. Bound in France.

ISBN : 1 930652 09 7

Humanoids Publishing™ and the Humanoids Publishing logo are trademarks of
Les Humanoïdes Associés S.A., Geneva (Switzerland), registered in various categories and countries.
Humanoids Publishing, a division of Humanoids Group.

4

YES... YOU SEE ME, NOW...

YOU ARE ME...

I AM YOU...

I AM YOURS...

MY VOW OF PEACE TOWARDS ALL THINGS FORBIDS ME TO KILL... I AM HERE TO HELP ALL BEINGS ATTAIN KNOWLEDGE... I AM HERE TO SAVE THEM... I CANNOT OBEY YOUR MOTHER, GABRIEL...

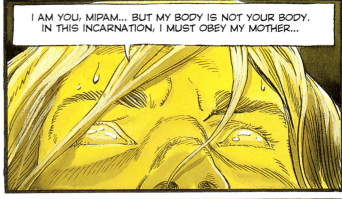

I AM YOU, MIPAM... BUT MY BODY IS NOT YOUR BODY. IN THIS INCARNATION, I MUST OBEY MY MOTHER...

I BEG YOU, GABRIEL... DO NOT MAKE ME BREAK THE LAWS OF HARMONY...

I HAVE NO CHOICE!... MY WHOLE PHYSICAL BEING RISES AGAINST YOU... I WAS FED ON ATMA'S MILK... IN THE NAME OF THIS FLESH, I ORDER YOU TO BECOME PART OF ME...

DISSOLVE INTO MY CELLS...

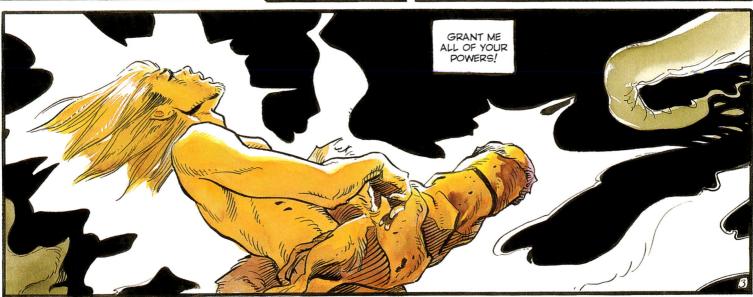

GRANT ME ALL OF YOUR POWERS!

5

YES! YES! THEY MUST ALL BE KILLED! WIPED OUT!

WHAT SHOULD WE DRINK TO NOW, GYALPO?

LET'S... HIC... TIP OUR BOWLS IN HONOR OF THE NEW DAY THAT IS BREAKING...

TO THE GLORY OF THE DAWN!

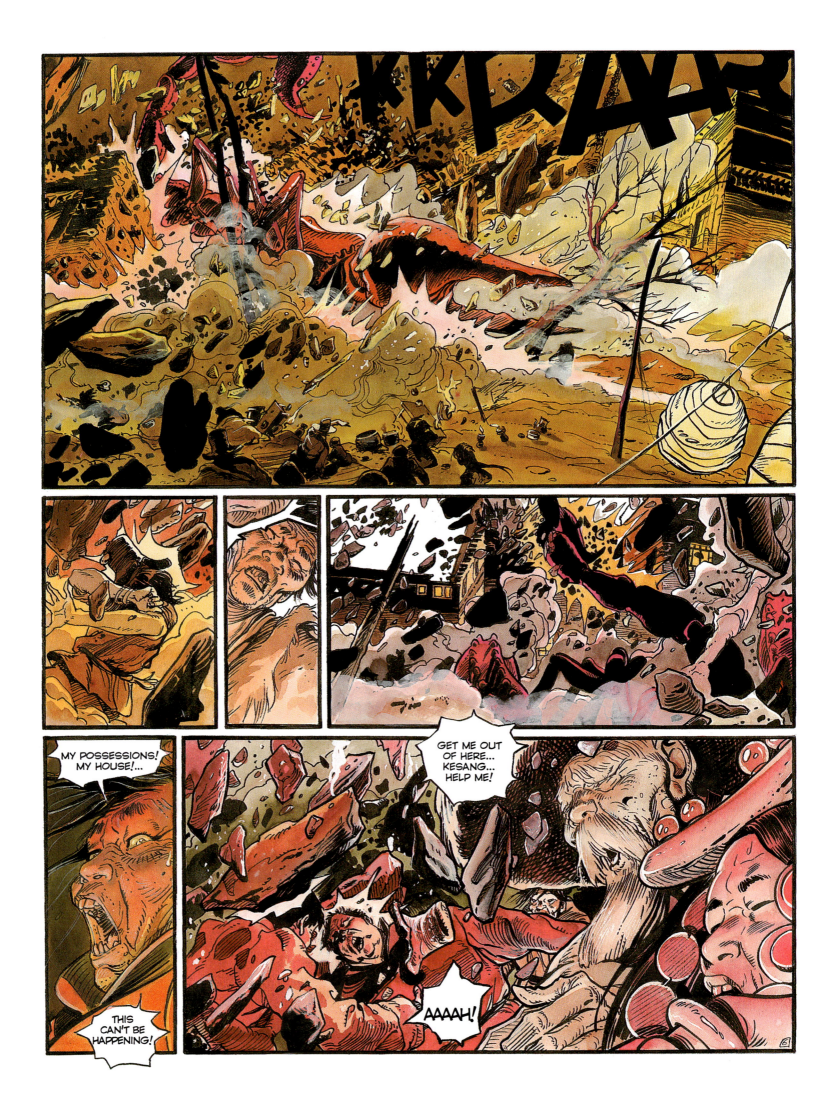

THE SCORPION MATCHES EACH OF GABRIEL'S MOVEMENTS WITH A MOVEMENT OF ITS OWN...

GABRIEL CAN COMMAND DEMONS! I KNEW IT! ONLY HE COULD AVENGE US!

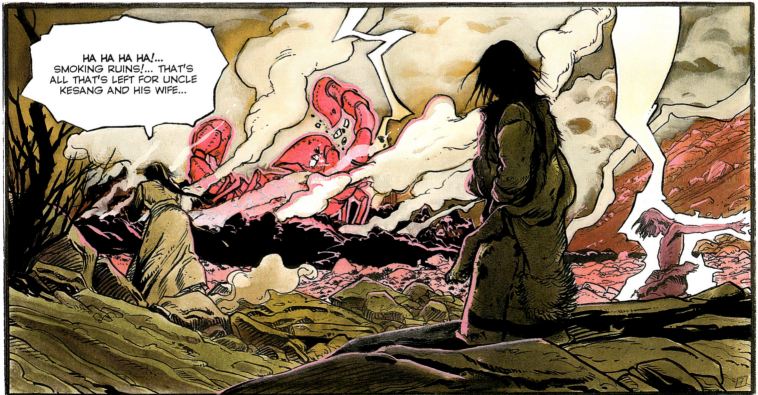

HA HA HA HA!... SMOKING RUINS!... THAT'S ALL THAT'S LEFT FOR UNCLE KESANG AND HIS WIFE...

9

14

15

17

THE EYE, WITH ITS DISCERNING POWERS, CAN SEE THINGS, BUT CANNOT SEE ITSELF...

FIRE CANNOT BURN ITSELF...

ON ITS OWN, THE SPIRIT CANNOT FIND THE SPIRIT...

!

voof...

VULTURE... WHY DO YOU DARE NOT KILL ME, SINCE THAT IS WHAT I DESIRE!?...

DO YOU THINK I'M ALIVE?!

WELL, YOU'RE WRONG! I AM A CORPSE!

EVERYTHING WITHIN ME IS DEAD... NOTHING EXISTS...

COME!

20

THAT
BRIDGE...

I... I'VE BEEN HERE
BEFORE... A LONG TIME
AGO...

21

22

OBSERVE WELL, FLESH-EATERS!... THIS CAVE WAS HIS ABODE...

TO ME, IT WILL SEEM BETTER THAN THE MOST LAVISH OF PALACES... IT WILL BE MY HOME...

FOR YEARS, HE ATE ONLY NETTLES... NOW I TOO WILL LIVE ONLY ON NETTLES...

AND I WILL CLOTHE MY BODY IN NOTHING BUT THICK COTTON FABRIC...

EVEN IF THE WORLD WERE FILLED WITH GOLD, A LIFE DEDICATED TO ATTAINING THE STATE OF ENLIGHTENMENT WOULD HAVE INFINITELY MORE VALUE...

OH, MY WELL-LOVED MASTER, GRANT ME YOUR BLESSINGS, SO THAT I MAY GROW... MAY I, THE VAGABOND, FIND A PERMANENT HOME IN SOLITUDE...

...SO THAT I MAY ACHIEVE THE SATISFACTION OF UNDERSTANDING MY TRUE SPIRIT...

IF I CRAVE MEAT, I'LL HAVE NETTLES, AND MORE NETTLES...

IF I CRAVE BARLEY, OR GRAINS, I'LL HAVE MORE NETTLES...

IF I CRAVE SALT, I'LL HAVE MORE NETTLES...

FROM THIS MOMENT FORTH, MY MANTRA SHALL BE: "ILLUSION... ALL IS BUT AN ILLU- SION..."

ILLUSION...
ALL IS BUT AN ILLUSION...

ILLUSION...
ALL IS BUT AN ILLUSION...

ILLUSION...
ALL IS BUT AN ILLUSION...

ILLUSION...
ALL IS BUT AN ILLUSION...

ILLUSION...
ALL IS BUT AN ILLUSION...

ILLUSION...
ALL IS BUT AN ILLUSION...

ILLUSION...
ALL IS BUT AN ILLUSION...

ILLUSION...
ALL IS BUT AN ILLUSION...

ILLUSION...
ALL IS BUT AN ILLUSION...

ILLUSION...
ALL IS BUT AN ILLUSION...

ILLUSION...
ALL IS BUT AN ILLUSION...

ILLUSION...
ALL IS BUT AN ILLUSION...

34

ILLUSION... ALL IS BUT AN ILLUSION... ILLUSION... ALL IS BUT AN ILLUSION... ILLUSION... ALL IS BUT AN ILLUSION... ILLUSION...

40

42

MEET FIRST TIME, AFTER DRAMATIC EVENTS... AH-IOU VERY YOUNG WHEN HUNTERS WOUND AH-IOU'S MOTHER... MOTHER DRAG SELF TO ISSIM'S HOME... IN MOUNTAINS...

SHE WATCH ISSIM, MANY YEARS... SHE KNOW YOUR GOODNESS... SHE LEAVES ONLY SON, AH-IOU... ME...

ISSIM TAKE CARE OF LITTLE ONE, ME GROW FOND ISSIM... LIVE LONG TIME TOGETHER... TAKE CARE EACH OTHER... ISSIM AH-IOU'S FATHER, MOTHER, CLOSEST FRIEND...

YOU TEACH AH-IOU TALK, AND EXPLAIN MYSTERIES ABOUT BEINGS OF YOUR SPECIES...

...AH-IOU LEARN THAT MEN LIVE VERY MUCH SHORTER LIVES THAN YETIS... AND ALAS, AH-IOU MAYBE ONLY YETI IN LAND OF SNOWS!

ISSIM REACH ENLIGHTENMENT FROM MEDITATION, AFTER MORE THAN SEVENTY YEARS BY MY SIDE...

AH-IOU TAKE CARE OF REMAINS, AND CREMATE... YOU MAKE VOW TO RETURN TO THIS WORLD TO HELP WORTHY SOULS REACH ENLIGHTENMENT...

SO AH-IOU RETREAT FOR FIRST TIME TO LONELY COLD OF HIGHEST PEAKS... WAIT FOR REBIRTH...

...MANY WINTERS PASS BEFORE YOU MONK AGAIN...

THEN FINALLY YOUR MEMORY OF PAST LIFE RETURN, COME LOOK FOR ME...

ISSIM REUNITE AH-IOU, GREAT JOY... YOU DIFFERENT... NEW FACE, NEW VOICE, NEW MOTIONS...

...BUT STILL SAME, INSIDE. SAME ESSENCE, SAME GOODNESS, SAME JOY IN YOU...

AND AH-IOU YOUR FRIEND AGAIN... YOUR NEW NAME: LOBSONG!...

KEEP GOING, AH-IOU... I'M... I'M STARTING TO REMEMBER...

...AFTER ISSIM, YOU ARE LOBSONG...

...THEN, NEXT LIFE, TSANGHA THAPA...

...THEN SONAM... MASTER SONAM, WHO LOVE ALL THINGS...

...THEN JAMAL, GREAT LAMA...

...THEN MIPAM, LATEST INCARNATION...

NOW AT LAST YOU COME... YOU TCHILINGA, GABRIEL MARPA...

AH-IOU WATCH YOU FROM AFAR, SINCE YOUR BIRTH, ISSIM... ALWAYS LOOK OUT FOR YOU... FROM FAR AWAY, AH-IOU WAIT...

46

47

TO BE CONTINUED IN "WATER TRIANGLE, FIRE TRIANGLE"

A. JODOROWSKY & G. BESS